P9-CMB-929

HARVEST HOME

JANE YOLEN ❧ ILLUSTRATED BY GREG SHED

SILVER WHISTLE / HARCOURT, INC. • *San Diego New York London* • *Printed in Singapore*

Three months just past, I helped to sow,
Bringing the harvest home.
I planted wheat in every row,
Bringing the harvest home.
Each tiny grain was set in earth
To give the wheat a wholesome berth.
A summer's coin, a year's full worth,
Bringing the harvest home.

But now we sweat beneath the sun,
Bringing the harvest home.
We work until the work is done,
Bringing the harvest home.
Above, the sky shines bright and blue;
The scythes swing high; our aim is true.
The downward swing cuts clean and through,
Bringing the harvest home.

I reap beside my brother, Ned,
Bringing the harvest home.
He is taller by a head,
Bringing the harvest home.
Though still young, we both work well
And need not ever rest a spell
(At least that anyone can tell).
Bringing the harvest home.

Two rows ahead, as in the past,
Bringing the harvest home,
Granddad and Pa are working fast,
Bringing the harvest home.
Gramps says to Dad, "The sun and rain
Were balanced well to grow our grain.
A goodly year. A goodly gain,
Bringing the harvest home."

Two rows behind work Ma and Jen,
Bringing the harvest home.
They cut more quickly than the men,
Bringing the harvest home.
We move as one on reaping day.
All time for work and none for play.
It cannot be another way,
Bringing the harvest home.

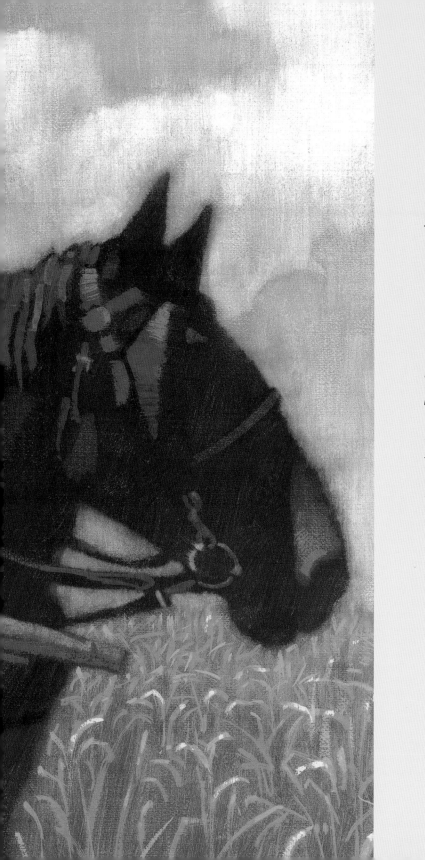

And up upon the wagon seat,
Bringing the harvest home,
Our grandma drives in all this heat,
Bringing the harvest home.
She clucks to Ginger and to Beau,
To haul the wagon row by row.
Not too quick and not too slow,
Bringing the harvest home.

The neighbors work our other field,
Bringing the harvest home.
They help us with the summer's yield,
Bringing the harvest home.
For just last week, in this same heat,
We helped our neighbors cut *their* wheat.
And now the circle is complete,
Bringing the harvest home.

Then just at noon, sun overhead,
Bringing the harvest home,
We stop to dine on cheese and bread,
Bringing the harvest home.
I look around at field and sky,
And at our neighbors so close by,
And think how lucky here am I,
Bringing the harvest home.

Ned grabs my hat and runs a row,
Bringing the harvest home.
He calls out, "Bess, you are too slow!"
Bringing the harvest home.
So I jump and follow fast.
The rows of waving grain are passed.
I catch Ned's shirttails near the last,
Bringing the harvest home.

Then side by side and hand in hand,
Bringing the harvest home,
We backtrack on our family land,
Bringing the harvest home.
The sun shines on each golden row,
While overhead a lazy crow
Keeps an eye on us below,
Bringing the harvest home.

And there already, blades swung high,
Bringing the harvest home,
Outlined against the blazing sky,
Bringing the harvest home,
Are Gramps and Dad, who, boy and man,
Have worked this way their whole lives' span,
Tied to the sun and rain and land,
Bringing the harvest home.

With aching back and blistered palms,
Bringing the harvest home,
With scythe still singing reapers' psalms,
Bringing the harvest home,
I look at Ned; he grins at me.
We nod and then swing mightily,
As if we felled a giant tree,
Bringing the harvest home.

We work the afternoon full out,
Bringing the harvest home.
I cut the last sheaf with a shout!
Bringing the harvest home.
Ma takes a twist of that last wheat
To make a harvest doll so neat,
With wheat gold hair and wheat gold feet,
Bringing the harvest home.

Jen sets the doll upon a pole,
Bringing the harvest home,
To represent the harvest soul,
Bringing the harvest home.
I hold the harvest pole up high
Beneath the fading harvest sky.
A skein of southbound geese flies by,
Bringing the harvest home.

Both Beau and Ginger in their stalls,
Bringing the harvest home,
Prick up their ears to fiddle calls,
Bringing the harvest home.
Our family the meal supplies—
Meats, salads, fruits, and pumpkin pies.
A feast beneath the harvest skies,
Bringing the harvest home.

And then we sing and dance and praise,
Bringing the harvest home.
To God the Sower prayers we raise,
Bringing the harvest home.
The golden crop is gathered in,
To store up summer in a bin.
Full thanks to all our friends and kin
For bringing the harvest home.

ABOUT HARVEST CUSTOMS

IN RURAL ENGLAND and Europe, as well as in many American farm communities, bringing the harvest home has always been a time of great celebration. Harvesters throughout the world have sung leader-chorus songs like *Harvest Home,* where one singer will sing the narrative line, and others will join in on the chorus: "Bringing the harvest home."

The harvest doll is another part of this celebration. Different countries have different names for this sheaf figure. In England it is a "corn dolly," because in England *corn* means "wheat." In Germany the figure is called Harvest Mother; in Prussia, Grandmother; in Denmark, Rye Woman or Old Barley Woman; and in Poland, Baba. Native Americans of the Northeast have made corn husk dolls since the beginning of corn agriculture, about seven centuries ago.

These days harvest dolls are no longer considered the spirit of the growing grain but are thought of as toys or ornaments. By following the instructions below, you can make your own harvest dolls of maize corn.

MATERIALS:

1–2 ears of corn with husks still on or 4 dried corn husks

4 cotton balls

scissors

string, cut into 10 pieces, long enough for tying around the corn husks

INSTRUCTIONS:

Remove four shucks or husks from the ears of corn and remove the corn silks. Discard the outer leaves. If using dried husks, soak them in warm water for at least half an hour. Longer is better. Fresh husks do not need soaking.

For each doll, take a strip of husk, put two of the cotton balls in the middle, and fold the husk in half. The cotton balls will become the doll's head; the loose ends of husk will become the doll's body and legs. Holding each end of the doll, twist the head around once or twice to form a neck. Tie the neck in place with a piece of string. The corn doll is begun.

To make the doll's arms, fold a second husk lengthwise and tie it near each end to form hands. Slip the tied corn husk between the loose ends of the husks under the head. Tie a string underneath the arms to hold them in place and to form a waist.

For the female corn doll, cut the husks of the body straight across at the bottom to form a skirt. For the male doll, divide the skirt into pants and tie at each ankle.

To Alison Isabelle Stemple, her book
—J. Y.

To Paulina
—G. S.

Text copyright © 2002 by Jane Yolen
Illustrations copyright © 2002 by Greg Shed

www.HarcourtBooks.com

Silver Whistle is a trademark of Harcourt, Inc., registered in the United States of America and/or other jurisdictions.

Library of Congress Cataloging-in-Publication Data
Yolen, Jane.
Harvest home/Jane Yolen; illustrated by Greg Shed.
p.   cm.
"Silver Whistle."
Summary: A young farm girl and her family bring in the new harvest and celebrate with prayers, songs, and a festive meal.
[1. Harvesting—Fiction.   2. Farm life—Fiction.   3. Stories in rhyme.]
I. Shed, Greg, ill.   II. Title.
PZ8.3.Y76Har   2002
[E]—dc21   98-40409
ISBN 0-15-201819-0

First edition
A C E G H F D B

The illustrations in this book were done in gouache on canvas.
The display type was set in Cancione.
The text type was set in Cloister Old Style.
Color separations by Bright Arts Ltd., Hong Kong
Printed and bound by Tien Wah Press, Singapore
This book was printed on totally chlorine-free Nymolla Matte Art paper.
Production supervision by Sandra Grebenar and Pascha Gerlinger
Designed by Trina Stahl